To Grace. The wonder of you is a constant reminder
that we are here . . . together . . . always. — T.C.

This book serves as evidence that we have
the courage to leave an imprint of wonder and
possibilities on this world and we will step
into the light and be counted. — B.C.

Text copyright © 2023 by Tami Charles • Illustrations copyright © 2023 by Bryan Collier • All rights reserved. Published by Orchard Books, an imprint of Scholastic Inc., *Publishers since 1920.* • ORCHARD BOOKS and design are registered trademarks of Watts Publishing Group, Ltd., used under license. SCHOLASTIC and associated logos are trademarks and/or registered trademarks of Scholastic Inc. • The publisher does not have any control over and does not assume any responsibility for author or third-party websites or their content. • No part of this publication may be reproduced, stored in a retrieval system, or transmitted in any form or by any means, electronic, mechanical, photocopying, recording, or otherwise, without written permission of the publisher. For information regarding permission, write to Scholastic Inc., Attention: Permissions Department, 557 Broadway, New York, NY 10012. • This book is a work of fiction. Names, characters, places, and incidents are either the product of the author's imagination or are used fictitiously, and any resemblance to actual persons, living or dead, business establishments, events, or locales is entirely coincidental. • Library of Congress Cataloging-in-Publication Data available • ISBN 978-1-338-75204-5 • 10 9 8 7 6 5 4 3 2 1   23 24 25 26 27 • Printed in China 38 • First edition, January 2023
Book design by Rae Crawford • The art for this book was created with collage and Winsor & Newton watercolor paint on 300lb. Arches watercolor paper.

WE ARE HERE

Illustrated by
Caldecott Honor Winner

Written by
Tami Charles

Bryan Collier

Orchard Books

New York
an imprint of Scholastic Inc.

The journey of who we are
stretches beyond
   rivers,
      roads,
mountains high-fiving
blue skies.

We were cool-like-that
from the beginning of time,
can't you see?

We are seeds,
you and me,

roots thick
 with dreams
  and stars
   and possibilities.

W

e turned
numbers to seasons
and patterns,
tracked moons in
outer space...

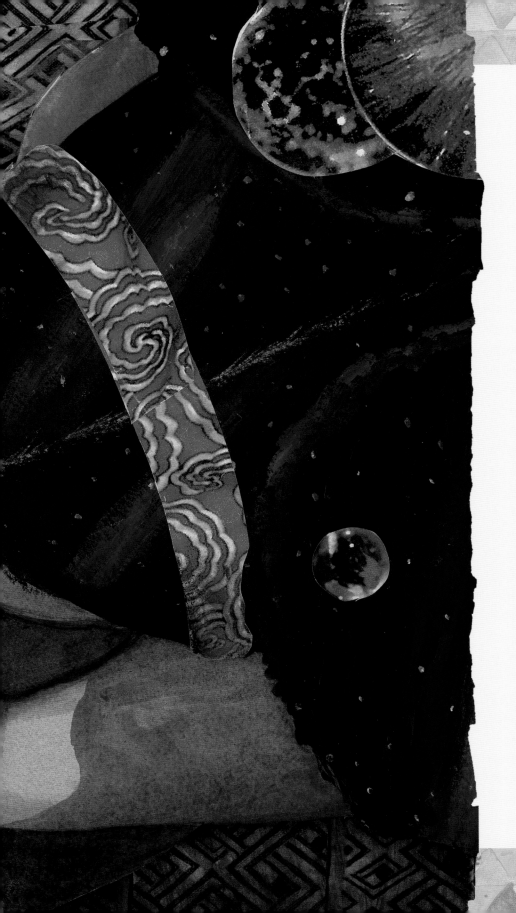

From brick and grit,
we built this place:
big hands,
small hands,
powerful in every way!

We are joy!
Igniting the world,
like stars caliente and bright,
like trumpets blaring at
midnight!

You hear that?
Skit-skat-
        caddy-wack!

It's the music of our past.
It's our rhythm
      and our blues
but you can't choose
(just one).

Our joy is the anthem of life
heard on monument steps,
opera stages,
stadiums filled with
thousands of faces . . .

It's in the spice of our isles,
the soul of our food
          feeding,
                    connecting
                              us across miles.

That joy, that wonder...
a burst of sunrays
laying the path
for today and always.

We are intercontinental,
can't you see?
With our strut,
and our style.

Trend-setters,
Go-getters,

Swagger that sweeps
across the globe!

We are . . .
multidialectal,
oh-so-intellectual.

One heart,
    uma alma . . .
un esprit . . .
    muchas lenguas.

We speak the language of
books and streets,
feet stamping concrete.

Countless steps
that set the world on fire
as we sing and chant
for all
to remember
our names.

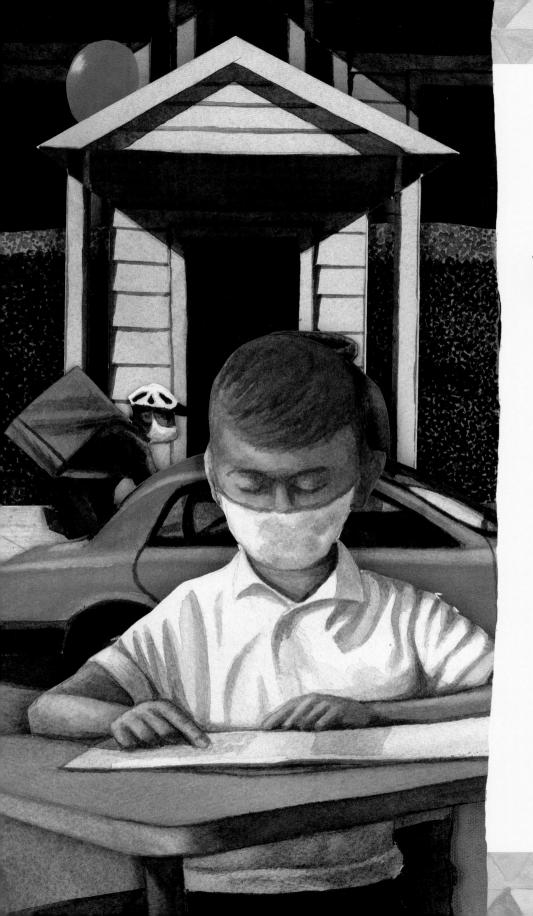

We are fearless,
more than we know.

When the world closed
its doors,
and worry set in,

there we were
putting on our capes,
springing to action again.

Why's that so?

**B**ecause
you and me,
we have always been heroes.

The same ones who
sat to take a stand,
the ones who ran
so we could fly...

So it's no surprise,
dear child,
we are all of these things,
and so much more ...

No matter what they say...

Because someday,
when it's your turn
to rule the world,

people will be amazed
and they will question
the power of you.

And when they do,
you be sure
to let them know . . .

You are
    brilliant,
        extraordinary,
            far-beyond-ordinary,

the very best of who we are.

Historic Figures and Contributions in *We Are Here*

Muddy Waters *(1913–1983)*: Born McKinley Morganfield, Muddy was an American blues singer and guitarist who is best known for his Chicago blues style, which mixed Mississippi blues with the electric guitar. Muddy earned six Grammy Awards during the span of his music career, including one for lifetime achievement in 1992.

Ella Fitzgerald *(1917–1996)*: American jazz singer, often called "First Lady of Song," Ella was the recipient of fourteen Grammy Awards, including one for lifetime achievement in 1967. She was the first woman to receive this award.

Howlin' Wolf *(1910–1976)*: Born Chester Arthur Burnett, Howlin' Wolf was a successful Chicago blues singer, harmonica player, and guitarist. In 2010, *Rolling Stone* magazine featured Howlin' Wolf in the "100 Greatest Artists of All Time," ranking him at number fifty-four.

Marian Anderson *(1897–1993)*: Marian broke barriers not only for African American concert vocalists but for all Black people in the United States. In 1939, when she was not allowed to perform at Constitution Hall in Washington, DC, because of her

race, many Americans were upset. Among them was Eleanor Roosevelt, the First Lady of the United States. The public outrage led to a new and even better opportunity for her—to sing on the steps of the Lincoln Memorial, where nearly 75,000 people came to listen and millions more heard her on the radio. Marian was awarded the Presidential Medal of Freedom in 1963, a National Medal of Arts in 1986, and a Grammy Lifetime Achievement Award in 1991.

Dr. Martin Luther King Jr. *(1929–1968)*: Leader of the civil rights movement in the United States, Dr. King delivered his famous "I Have a Dream" speech on the steps of the Lincoln Memorial on August 28, 1963. In 1964, he was awarded the Nobel Peace Prize. Fun fact: Across the globe are more than 1,000 streets named in honor of Dr. King for his hard work to create equality for people of all races, backgrounds, and faiths.

Foods: Many global cuisines feature foods from the African diaspora. For example, the coffee plant originated in Ethiopia. Plantains, often featured in many Caribbean dishes, originated in Asia, but were brought to

Africa through trade. Explorers then brought plantains to the Americas.

Fashion: From cornrows to herringbone chains, dashiki prints and elegant swing dresses, Black fashions have made a statement for centuries. Being recognized for our work, however, has not always been easy. For example, Anne Lowe never received credit for designing the wedding dress of Jacqueline Bouvier, whose first husband, John F. Kennedy, would become the thirty-fifth president of the United States. Fortunately, Black-owned fashion brands such as FUBU and Cross Colours would years later explode onto the fashion scene and set global trends.

GLOSSARY

Caliente *(kah-LYEHN-teh)*: Spanish for "hot"

Uma alma *(OOM-ahl-muh)*: Brazilian Portuguese for "one soul"

Un esprit *(uhn ess-PREE)*: French for "one spirit"

Muchas lenguas *(MOO-chas LAYN-gwas)*: Spanish for "many tongues," meaning multiple languages

AUTHOR'S NOTE

For a long time, I have wanted to write something in honor of my daughter, whom I didn't get to meet. When the global pandemic occurred, coupled with the horrific acts of injustice against people of color like George Floyd, I began to wonder: How would I have shown my daughter this world? How would I prepare her to face it?

This is how *We Are Here* was born—from a dire need to drown out the hatred with something far more powerful: love.

If *All Because You Matter* was an affirmation, then *We Are Here* is a celebration! In my heart, I know there is one more missing piece of the puzzle . . . the confirmation. A forthcoming third book in the series, *United Together*, forms a complete, unified thought and seeks to affirm, celebrate, and confirm the power and greatness that lie within all our children.

We Are Here is for my daughter, Grace, and the wonder of who she could have been and of what this world could be. It's for the joy I would have shown her, the beauty and excellence of our ancestors I would have taught her. We come from a civilization who built ancient places, like Benin City, with their own hands; whose early scientific discoveries led to the creation of the 365-day calendar and even the world's first astronomical site! We sing like Mahalia Jackson and Marian Anderson, win Olympic gold medals like Constantin Henriquez de Zubiera, spark movements with poetry like Jason Reynolds, Jacqueline Woodson, and Elizabeth Acevedo.

We are here. We have *always* been here—influencing and contributing our gifts to the world, for all to see and enjoy. As a mom, these words are my gift to Grace, to my son, Christopher, and to all children who need to hear them.

Our children represent the very best of who we are and the legacy from which they come. Their joy is our protest.

ILLUSTRATOR'S NOTE

In the process of creating a visual storyline for this project, I looked to a painting from one of my favorite artists, John Biggers, who painted multiple shotgun houses much like the one in Georgia he was raised in.

I thought these row houses could serve as a timeline by which I could document important markers in history, such as cultural innovations ranging from the African drums to blues, jazz, rap, and hip-hop. Also woven in is the history of protest and struggle for equality for all and fair treatment under the law. And in the end, you will see that we are one great big community and that this is the evidence, with our fists thrust to the sky, shouting: WE ARE HERE!!!